The Crystallizer

In another dastardly plot to defeat MASK, Miles Mayhem threatens to turn all unprotected life into crystal!

© 1986 Kenner Parker Toys Inc. (KPT). All rights reserved.
Published in Great Britain by World International Publishing Limited.
An Egmont Company, Egmont House, P.O. Box 111,
Great Ducie Street, Manchester M60 3BL.
Printed in Italy. SBN 7235 8817 1.
1st reprint 1987.

THE
CRYSTALLIZER

"VENOM have stolen a top secret weapon — the Crystallizer — which can turn people into crystal," explained Matt Trakker to his team of MASK agents. "It's our job to stop them using it." Moments later, the agents were placing their repowered masks on their heads. "Let's go," Matt said.

As the agents moved towards their vehicles, they were stopped by Matt's son, Scott. "Can I come too, Dad?" he said.

"No, it's too dangerous," Matt replied, secretly smiling at his son's bravery.

"Gee, T-Bob, Dad never takes me anywhere," Scott complained.

"I don't know, Scott," said T-Bob, "from what I know of the mission it is dangerous ... very dangerous."

"The mission can't be that dangerous," Scott shouted, "so I'm going anyway."

"I don't think you should . . ." began T-Bob worriedly, but Scott had already raced off along the corridor.

T-Bob easily caught up with Scott and decided that for Scott's safety he had better go along with him. Moments later they were speeding along the highway. "I checked out the details on the MASK computer," Scott said as they travelled along. "I'm going to show Dad that I'm not a kid anymore."

Meanwhile, Miles Mayhem, the leader of the evil organisation VENOM, was talking with his aide, Dagger. "This Crystallizer is the weapon with which we will defeat MASK!"

Mayhem smiled evilly as he continued. "This device will turn all unprotected life into crystal. We will then threaten to destroy them unless MASK surrenders to me."

"That's perfect blackmail, Mayhem," Dagger said with glee.

Scott Trakker had just arrived in the town when suddenly he found he could not move! "Oh no!" T-Bob shouted. "This is VENOM's work. Now what can I do?"

Above the town, on the hill, Mayhem sneered. "Let's see MASK solve this . . . if they can get past my trap!"

Further down the highway Mayhem's trap snapped shut as a massive explosion ripped open the highway right in front of the MASK agents. "Emergency avoidance!" Matt yelled, and the intended victims swerved with well practised ease to avoid the killer blast.

"Mayhem's playing for keeps," Sato said to Matt as they drew close to the town.

"Well, Spectrum warned us that it might be a trap and as usual they were right," Matt replied as the vehicles slowed down and the drivers prepared for anything that VENOM might throw at them.

As the Rhino moved closer to the town the dashboard data-screen showed static and then slowly came back to life . . . and the face of Mayhem glared out at them. "I have turned all the townspeople into crystal. Unless you hand over your masks in one hour I will destroy them all," he threatened.

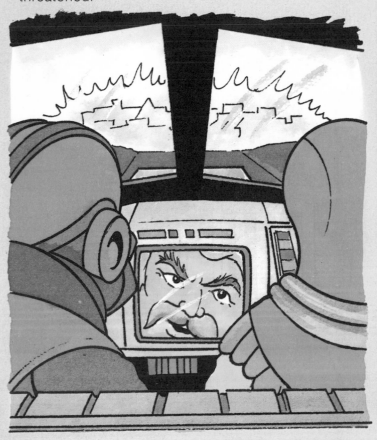

"Look for yourselves," Mayhem continued as the screen changed to show several people who had been turned into crystal. Matt was shocked to see that one of the victims was Scott! "You have one hour," Mayhem repeated as the screen went dead.

Matt ordered his team-mates out of their vehicles. "Any sound we make could shatter one of those crystal people," he said.

"Just like glass breaking in a shock wave," Sato added.

"Exactly," said Matt, "so we must continue on foot."

"If they harm one hair on my son's head . . ." Matt
began.

"Don't worry, Matt," said Sato, reassuringly.

"Sato's right, Matt," Hawks added. "MASK is here
now and that's always bad news for VENOM."

Matt prayed that his friend was right.

"Our masks will protect us from the rays," Matt reasoned, "so it's up to us to get that weapon and change these innocent people back to normal." As they walked along the streets Matt couldn't help thinking about his son and what he would do to Mayhem if Scott was harmed.

Not far away, in a nearby street, Dagger had spotted T-Bob. I'll take care of him, he thought as a fiery jet shot from his mask, hitting the metal droid.

"So, MASK think they can defeat me with a child's toy, do they?" Mayhem gloated.

"Say boss, does this mean that MASK are finished?" Dagger asked.

Mayhem laughed and replied in a cold, hard voice, "Soon. Very soon."

Unknown to VENOM, Buddie Hawks had been spying on them through the window. Having heard everything he needed, he ran back to his team-mates. It took only moments to explain what had happened. "Now that we know where VENOM are we can put my plan into effect," Matt said and outlined his plan to his friends.

Minutes later, Matt used his Ultra Flash Mask to create a blinding light in the street. As VENOM ran out to investigate, Hawks used his Penetrator Mask to slip through the wall and into the room where the Crystallizer was kept. As soon as Hawks entered the room he could see where the Crystallizer was housed.

Knowing that he hadn't a second to lose, Hawks dashed across the room and deactivated the evil device. Immediately, the low hum stopped sounding from the machine. The people should change back now . . . which means we can use our masks without any fear, thought Hawks as he made for the door.

Outside, a fierce battle raged between MASK and VENOM. The streets were filled with the eerie sounds of the super-masks as flashes and blasts shot from either side of the street. The noise began to attract the recently freed townspeople, who came to investigate.

"There he is," shouted one of the leaders of the townspeople as he pointed at Mayhem. Suddenly, the angry population burst into the street and began to chase the evil warlord back to his waiting Switchblade. Behind him, an equally scared Dagger ran towards his Jackhammer.

Within moments Mayhem and Dagger had made it to their escape vehicles and fled the scene.

"Gee, Dad," Scott said to his happy father, "I'm sorry for doing what I did."

"You should never do anything on your own," Matt replied. "Parents tell kids to behave to protect them, not to hurt them."

Matt could tell by the look in his son's eyes that he had learnt his lesson.

"At least we stopped VENOM," Sato said.

"Yes," agreed Matt, "and we will continue to stop them and foil their evil plans, especially when they threaten the freedom of innocent people."